Muffy Mac Mouse
Comes to
PARAGON PARK

By Kate MacLeod Emery
with Illustrations by Rich Daley

To
Isla & Gavin,
Enjoy!
Miss Kate

Kate MacLeod Emery

Dedication

It is with great admiration and gratitude that I dedicate this book to the "Friends of the Paragon Carousel". This non-profit organization was formed by a gathering of many amazing and caring people from the Town of Hull, Massachusetts. This group of wonderful people gave the town the precious gift of the 1928 Philadelphia Toboggan Company carousel. This beautiful antique carousel, with the musical Wurlitzer Band Organ, was the most beautiful of all the rides, once located in the center of Paragon Park. This dedicated organization keeps the horses flying and the music flowing, entertaining everyone from near and far away.

Acknowledgments

My first thanks and praise will always be to the Lord. With the gift of writing He has given me, I was able to create Muffy MacMouse. I also thank him for the gift of spending the autumn days of my life with Lloyd, my husband extraordinaire. He has taken my days from black and white to magnificent color, filling each day walking beside me down this exciting path.

To my amazing illustrator, Rich Daley, who was able to bring us back in time to walk down Nantasket Ave. and into Paragon Park by putting us into the dream of a grand holiday affair. Our grand-children along with our son, Brian, join us once again as the characters in this book.

To Cynthia Rizzo, a very special friend, who as a Master of Grammar herself, helped me to master mine, my sincere thanks.

My sincere thanks to my talented nephews, David, Donald and Scott Main, for arranging and performing the songs on the CD.

In appreciation to the Stone family who operated Paragon Park for sixty years, thanks for the memories.

Our sincere thanks to the Friends of the Carousel for being so kind and gracious to us, by giving us the opportunity to spread the word about caring, sharing and making good choices to the many wonderful children who enter this magical place to ride the ponies. For the year 2015, Muffy MacMouse will return again as one of the adopted horses, number 7B on the Paragon Carousel.

nce upon a time there was a magical and enchanting place called Paragon Park that was located along the shores of the Atlantic Ocean. The park was at Nantasket Beach in the beautiful seaside town of Hull Massachusetts.

Paragon Park opened in the year 1905 bringing fun and happiness to many children and their families. Over the years many of the rides and attractions would change, but everyone experienced the thrill of these exciting rides and the prizes they could win. In 1928, a beautiful Philadelphia Toboggan Company carousel with hand carved horses appeared in the center of the park. The sound of the Wurlitzer Band Organ on the carousel thrilled many people strolling through the park. After the excitement of the rides and the games, the children would race to the beach for one last swim before losing high tide and heading for home.

On a sad day, in the year 1984, it was announced that Paragon Park would be closing, leaving everyone with just memories. In 1986, the Paragon Carousel was bought at an auction and moved to its present location on Nantasket Avenue. In 1996, a group of caring people from the town of Hull rescued the Paragon Carousel from a second auction. The group formed a non-profit organization called "Friends of the Paragon Carousel." This organization has given everyone a chance once again to enjoy this beautiful carousel that will be celebrating its 90th birthday in 2018.

In this book, Muffy MacMouse will take his friends from the Village of Friendship into a dream that will take them on a journey back in time. The dream will give them the gift of reliving the memories of Paragon Park that many of us have carried along for so many years. Muffy hopes that all his readers will also come along in the dream to enjoy riding the rides, strolling along Nantasket Avenue, tasting salt water taffy, frozen custard and cotton candy. At the end of their dream, Muffy and his friends will continue up Nantasket Avenue to the new location of the Paragon Carousel, hopping on their ponies and riding up and down into the future.

COME ONE COME ALL

A SURPRISE MEETING WILL BE HELD ON THE VILLAGE GREEN AT ONE O'CLOCK

"Hello all my wonderful friends in the village," said Muffy. "Thank you for coming to this special meeting. I want to thank you for showing me all about caring and sharing with my brothers and sisters. I have learned so much from your examples and I am still working on sharing my marshmallows!! I have planned a fun vacation for all of you to show you how much I appreciate all you have done for me. We will be leaving tomorrow morning."

"Where are we going?" they asked.

Muffy told them, "I will be taking you to my special home away from the Village, a beautiful seaside town called Hull, which is in Massachusetts. We will be staying at the Clock Tower Inn. During our sleep we will all go into a dream, taking us back in time to enjoy the memories of Paragon Park of long ago. Then the last place that I will take you will be to my beloved Paragon Carousel."

"Yea!!!!" they all shouted.

"Oh, my!" said Muffy, "Why are you crying Miss Krista Tree? You look so sad."

"I won't be able to go to Paragon Park with everybody because my roots are planted in the ground," said Miss Krista Tree.

"You will be able to come to the park. We will wrap up your roots and bring you in our new trailer," said Muffy.

All in a Dream

Kate MacLeod Emery

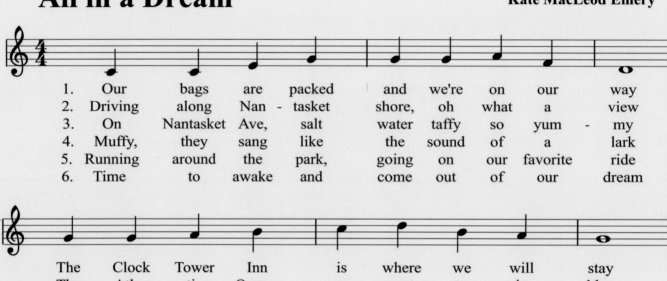

1. Our bags are packed and we're on our way
2. Driving along Nan - tasket shore, oh what a view
3. On Nantasket Ave, salt water taffy so yum - my
4. Muffy, they sang like the sound of a lark
5. Running around the park, going on our favorite ride
6. Time to awake and come out of our dream

The Clock Tower Inn is where we will stay
The Atlan - tic Ocean, so pret - ty in blue
What a perfect snack for my little tum - my
There's the big yellow ent - rance to Paragon Park
We took our last swim before losing high tide
We'll always re - member the sights we have seen

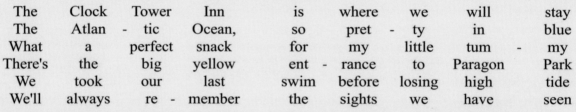

The old red Bent - ley chug - ging al - ong route 3A
As we walk together we are friends thro - ugh and through
The fluffy cotton can - dy color - ed pur - ple and pink
The gia - nt roller - coaster ris - ing high in the sky
We thanked our new friends as we bid them fare - well
Cotton candy salt - water taffy and van - illa ice cre - am

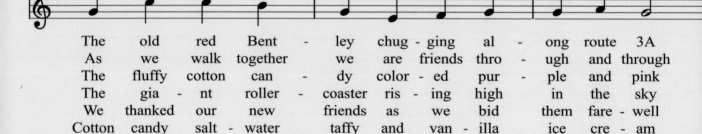

Ov - er the bridge we go head - ing for Nan - tasket bay
Are we asleep in a dream, could all this magic be true?
What fla - vor do I want, let me think, let me think
Shall we be brave and go on this ride, you and I
Our best ride of all was on the Para - gon Caro - usel
We head back to the Village and the end of our dream

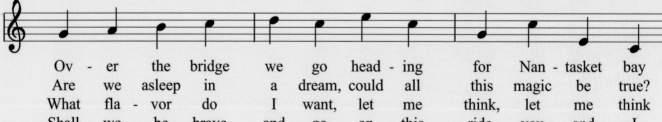

"Yippee!!! We're on our way to Paragon Park," they all shouted.
"Hang on," said Muffy, "this will be a wonderful vacation for everyone. I promise!!"

TO PARAGON
PARK OR BUST

"Oh! The Clock Tower Inn is very beautiful," said Sarah Bella.
"Is that our room way up in the very top of the clock tower?" asked Katie T[...]
"Don't worry Katie Tiptoe," said Geno the Giraffe, "I will stretch my neck b[...]
clock tower and will take everyone to the [...]
Nathaniel Bob dresses Miss Krista Tr[...]
Christmas lights and puts her t[...]

"What will happen in the morning when they see Krista Tree all lit up?" asked Ashley Apple Muffin. "Well that's our big surprise," said Mayor Robert, "we will give our wonderful new friends the gift of CHRISTMAS IN JULY."
"WHAT A GREAT IDEA," they all shouted.

he squeeze onto my neck and
the Giraffe.

onquil. "We have made our
Geno's neck."

Tiptoe.
side the
top while
ee with
bed."

"Good night every one," said Muffy.
"We will wake up early tomorrow morning and go for a swim at Nantasket Beach."
"When can we go inside the Paragon Carousel?" cried Johnny the Jester.

"We will not go inside the carousel until the
last night of our vacation," said Muffy.
"You must learn to be patient and wait
for the BIG SURPRISE!!!"

"HI- HO, HI-HO, it's off to the beach we go!" they all sang.

There are some safety rules that I want you all to learn when you are at the beach," Muffy told them. "You should never stand with your back to the ocean as the waves can get very big!"

"Oh, Muffy!!" they all hollered. "Are you ok? The rules are also for you to learn."
"I know," said Muffy, "I will remember to do what I ask others to do and we will always be safe."

"Oh my! Muffy," said Ashley Apple Muffin, "You would not be in so much trouble if you would only follow the rules! You must practice what you preach at the beach," she told him.

"Well, I can hardly wait to try one of those Kohr's frozen custard cones," said Nathaniel Bob.

"Oh, Muffy, that big red clown nose fits you perfectly," said Ashley Apple Muffin. "This pink cotton candy is simply delicious," said Princess Claudia. "I have never tasted anything like this," said Lord James.

"My, oh, my, oh, my! This is soooooo yummy for my little tummy," said Leah Lady Slipper to Johnny the Jester. This is quite a treat that we will always remember."

"HOORAY," they all shouted, "we are finally here at the Paragon Park. OH! What fun we will have riding on all those wonderful rides."
"Okay," said Muffy, "follow me and remember to obey the rules in the park."

"Wheeeeeeeeeeee, this is great," they all shouted.
"Is anybody afraid to go on this ride?" asked Muffy. "Now is your chance to get off."
"WHAT?" said Geno the Giraffe. "Do you think that we're a bunch of babies?
BRING IT ON!!"

"WOW !! This is great," said Muffy. "What is there to be afraid of?"
"What is all the hype about?" yelled Geno the Giraffe.
"This ride is a piece of cake," said Deeje the Dinosaur.
"This isn't even worth a bark," woofed B.J.
"Hang on everyone," said Muffy, "HERE WE GO!!!!!"

"HELLO? Where is everyone?" questioned Muffy. "Is anybody here? Is anybody going to answer me? Am I here in the dark alone with all these ghosts?"

THE RED MILL

"Well, that was no fun!! We just had our Saturday night bath and had our hair fixed and we looked so beautiful," said Nicola Bell.
"Oh no," cried Deeje the Dinosaur, "their hair will never be the same!!"

"PEEK–A-BOO!!!!" they all sang out to the people.
"This is so exciting," said Sara Bella.
"It's like camping under a tent," said Nicola Bell.

"If you put us together we will be four feet tall," cried B.J. "Please won't you let us go on the Bumper cars, they are my favorite amusement ride in the entire park. We promise to be very careful."

"Well, if you promise to be very careful," said the worker, "I will let you go on the ride."

"GREAT!!"said B.J. "Hop on my back Bristal the Crystal Angel!"

"WOW," said Nathaniel Bob, "what was that?" "Yea!!" they all shouted.
"That was Bristal the Crystal Angel's glowing halo," said B.J. "She lit up the whole place."
"That was pretty cool," said Joshua Polywog.

"Wheeeee.
It's so much fun swinging
on the Lindy Loop,"
said Princess Claudia.
"I just love rocking back and forth.
We may never get off this ride,"
said Jilly Jonquil and Leah Lady Slipper.

"You've got to be kidding,"
said Geno the Giraffe.
"Wow, was that my neck
whipping bye?"

"My friends," said Muffy, "that is James with Lola, the lead horse on the Carousel. James restores all the horses in his workshop and makes them so beautiful. This is John and Marie, they take wonderful care of the Paragon Park Museum, giving people the thrill of looking back on pleasant memories. Marie is president of Friends of the Carousel."

"Muffy, your friends are very colorful," said Marie.

"Hi Karen," said Muffy. "My friends would like to say hello."

"Well, hello," said Karen. "I welcome people into the museum, would you like to come in?"

"Oh, yes, we would love to," everyone said.

"Hello, Miss Patti, these are my friends from the village," said Muffy.

"Hello Miss Patti," his friends sang out.

"Well, hello back," Patti called out! "I am very happy to meet you all. I hope you are having a great time."

"We are having a splendid time," said Geno the Giraffe.

"We are finally going to see the Carousel tonight," said Miss Ashley Apple Muffin.

"I can certainly tell that you all like the ice cream from our Creamery," said Patti.

"We just love it," they all shouted.

"WOW!!!! It's all so beautiful," they all sing
out in a chorus!!
"I have never seen anything so wonderful," cried
Leah Lady Slipper. "This picture will stay in my
memory forever."
"Thanks Muffy, for taking us to this beautiful place,"
said Jilly Jonquil.

The Carousel

Kate MacLeod Emery

1. Go - ing up up up and com - ing down down down
2. The spiral poles are go - ing up and com - ing down
3. There are forty two jump - ers pran - cing oh so high
4. Child - ren sing - ing to the band organ mel - o - dy

The fly - ing horses are spin - ing arou - nd and around
The smo - oth sil - ver poles going arou - nd and around
Twen - ty four stand - ers racing arou - nd and flying by
Their voices sound - ing like ang - els in perfect harm - ony

Mount your po - ny and at the sound of the bell
Lola wear - ing her P T C shi - eld so well
Sixty - six horses are paint - ed bright col - ors so well
To the beat of the drums, the pipes and the bell

Your ride will start on the Par - a - gon Car - ou - sel
Lead - ing her horses on the Par - a - gon Car - ou - sel
Swirling us arou - nd on the Par - a - gon Car - ou - sel
Till we ride again on the Par - a - gon Car - ou - sel

Everyone chimes out, "Thank you all so very much for making our
vacation to Paragon Park and the Paragon Carousel so grand."

Everyone agreed, "It has been a week of majestic memories that we will take back to our little village and keep them in our hearts forever."

"So long everybody," they all shout out!! "The presents under the tree are for all of you from all of us. Merry, Merry, Christmas in July. We won't say good-by, because we will be back."

Till then